Mike's Coffee

A Syllble Studios Collaboration

By
Taiwo Adesina
Valeria Lake
Brittney Jones

Syllble Studios

Copyright © 2018 by Syllble, Inc.

Acknowledgment

The writers gratefully acknowledge Paul Russell and David Russell for their guidance, encouragement and editorial expertise in produce this Syllble Studios Novel.

Contents

PART 1: CVS

Winn

Winn James had been waiting for her in the parking lot for two hours. Immediately after work, he had driven to the Washington Street CVS, the one wedged between Pop's liquor store and Min's Nails, and now just sat in his old Accord, waiting. Lonni had told him a couple weeks ago that she might be pregnant, and the awkward silence since then was finally overwhelming him. They were trapped in the car together – him and the silence. It had invited itself in and sat down in the passenger's seat, staring at him, making him think things just by the nature of its presence. He sat there and endured it. Welcomed it. He looked out his window to avert its gaze.

It was approaching 7 p.m. and already getting dark. Only trace elements of Philadelphia's evening rush hour traffic remained, and the number of pedestrians had dwindled. Normal families - normal people! - were in their homes now, gathering around dinner tables or populating restaurants, communing with loved ones, sharing the adventures, challenges and highlights of their day. Reflecting, fellowshipping, unloading. He felt lonely. All he had was the silence that enveloped the sedan, and the promise of an imminent battle with Lonni.

A couple of about 18 months, they had discussed the possibility of a life together and the prospects of a family. Winn knew he wanted a large family because he was an only child, and the path towards securing lifelong friends had been challenging for him. With siblings, you were guaranteed, to a certain extent, a group of people that loved you and would show up for you no matter what. People who knew your story, not because you told them, but because they were there when it was unfolding. Sometimes they even knew the narrative better than you.

Winn wanted a vibrant household. He wanted every breakfast to feel like brunch at McKinney's, and every dinner to be a feast. He wanted ballet lessons, basketball camps and sleepovers. He wanted the pride, the rewards, and the messiness that came with being a parent. But he didn't want it now. It was simple - he was not prepared. When Lonni called him two weeks ago saying she thought she might be pregnant, he was literally speechless.

"Hello?" she'd asked again, and he could hear the anxiety in her voice. "Are you there?"

Winn cleared his throat, "Yes, I am. Sorry. Uhhh, how do you know? Did you, umm, take a test or something?"

"No. I just…know." Her voice was softer.

"Oh, well, do you want to take a test?"

"I do, but…I'm afraid. I'll give it a couple weeks and see how I feel or see if my period comes."

"Can you do that?"

"What do you mean?"

"Can you just do nothing? Is that healthy for the baby?"

"We don't even know if there's a baby," Lonni snapped.

"Well, shouldn't we try to know right away?" There was a brief pause. He wasn't sure if he'd said the wrong things. Should he have congratulated her? Should he have sounded more concerned or happier? What does one do at a time like this? He thought that years of watching television and films, reading books and magazines, or merely going through life, would prepare him for a time like this, but they didn't.

No one and nothing can prepare a person for the announcement of an unplanned pregnancy. Aside from that, he didn't know the basics of the female anatomy, or of pregnancy or childbirth. He'd heard that prenatal vitamins, books, and a specialized type of yoga were involved, but that was the extent of it. He wasn't sure what was supposed to happen, and at what stages these happenings were supposed to begin. He hated his ignorance at that moment; and frankly the ignorance he'd gotten away with for most of his life.

"I think I just need to wait," she finally said, decisively.

Winn had respected and appreciated her decision. Even though he was two years younger than Lonnie, he often felt that he was the mature one. At the time, he felt he couldn't bear knowing right away, and he did not want to be in the position of telling her what to do. They'd barely spoken in the past two weeks; their limited exchanges centering around the mundane, each afraid to address the huge bomb that had gone off in the middle of their lives.

Last night, Lonni had texted him asking him to meet her here after work. He knew she got off at 5:30, but he was grateful for the delay. He didn't even press her about it. He needed more time, even with the with silence, to gather his thoughts. He realized then that he had no idea if Lonni wanted this. He knew what he wanted; the intervening weeks helped him figure that out. But he had no sense of what she was feeling, or even what she was going through.

Moments later, he was blinded by the headlights of her trusty Corolla as she pulled into the parking lot. She parked across from him, even though there were a few spaces next to his car. He saw her open the door and get out of the car before she turned it off - a weird habit of hers. She was wearing an oversized t-shirt and jeans, and her purse was slung over her shoulder. Her dark brown hair was pulled into a bun on atop her head, but a few stray ringlets fell to frame her face. He hadn't seen her in two weeks and she looked beautiful to him.

Suddenly, the back door of the car opened and what appeared to be a six or seven-year-old girl jumped out. She was smiling, as she slammed the door shut and turned to look at Lonni. *What was going on?*

He got out of the car and waved. Lonni waved back but it a quick, impersonal gesture. It was the wave equivalent of being dismissive with someone. She wasn't smiling as she took the girl's hand. At 5'-4" she towered over the small girl. He thought that's how we must look when we walk together.

"Hey," he said offering her a quick hug, "Who do we have here?"

She sighed impatiently. "This is Tyra, my neighbors' kid."

"I'm Tyra!" she squealed. Her brown curly hair was parted in two sections and bounced to reflect her enthusiasm.

He laughed, "Hello Tyra, very nice to meet you."

He looked at Lonni, anticipating further explanation which she did not provide. "Shall we?" she said.

"After you."

They walked into the CVS where Lonni beelined towards the Feminine Care section. He had the sneaky feeling she'd been there before, scoping out the options, debating if she should "just buy it, damn it!" He walked quickly to keep up while trying to stay out of the wandering eyesight of Tyra. She was trailing slowly behind them, looking around like she'd never been in a drugstore before. He couldn't blame her. The Washington Avenue CVS was massive, the largest in North Philly, supplying almost every consumer good one could think of. He didn't frequent it often, but the few times he'd shopped there he'd been impressed by its size. He looked back again, and Tyra had stopped to look at the crayons and markers in the back-to-school section. He decided she'd be fine, and soon caught up with Lonni. She was already reading the back of a small purple box and had a pink one in her other hand.

"Hey," he said, placing a hand on the small of her back. "How have you been?"

"Fine. Really," she mumbled, not looking up.

"Lonni, please, let's try to talk this through. What has been going on with you? I haven't seen you two weeks."

"Well, a lot has been happening," she said, looking up at him. "I'm obviously pregnant for starters." He hated her sarcasm.

"What's up with the five-year-old?"

"She's six. She's Angela's kid."

"Who?"

"From next door. You know, the black divorcee with the Hispanic ex-husband."

"Who?"

"Never mind." He felt like he should know who she was talking about, but he didn't. And he didn't really care. She had talked about all her neighbors at one point or another, but they were a blur to him.

"Anyway, have you thought about what you'd do if the test came back positive?" he asked. Lonni sighed and shrugged, then placed the purple box back on the shelf.

"All I know is I want to buy this, get the child home, and take the test."

He'd read online last week about how to be a supportive father by being sensitive to what she's feeling, without losing one's place in the decision process at the time.

"Okay," he said, "Then let me pay for the test".

Tyra was still in the next aisle over, and he was grateful she was far enough away not to have heard their conversation, but close enough that they didn't have to hunt her down.

He could be wrong, but it seemed that the pimply-faced cashier was judging them as he paid for the test. His cheeks warmed up and suddenly felt ashamed that he felt that way.

Winn followed the silver Toyota back to Lonni's house. After they pulled into the driveway, she took Tara by the wrist while unzipping her pink backpack with her other hand. He didn't know what had transpired between the two of them in the car, but Lonni was irate and Tyra had tears streaming down her face.

"I'm coming," Tara said, brushing past him.

Lonni's place was a bit of a mess, but he wasn't surprised. She was not the most organized person. Tyra immediately dropped her backpack by the front door on a pile of Lonni's shoes and ran to the TV.

Lonni ignored her and summoned Winn to follow her to her bedroom.

"What was that all about?" he asked, shutting her door.

"It's nothing," she said, reaching into her bag for the pink box that would determine their future. "She's just…her." She smiled at him, but he could tell there was no emotion there.

"I'm going to go pee on this thing," she said, waving the box. "Make yourself comfortable. It shouldn't take too long."

As the bathroom door shut, he sat on the edge of her unmade bed. There were clothes all over the floor; heels, tennis shoes and flats strewn everywhere. Her room looked like it belonged to someone who decided what to wear by trying on every piece of clothing, every day. She had a window-facing table where countless makeup items surrounded her laptop.

"Is the type of woman you raise a child with?" he asked himself. But immediately he felt guilt at his train of thought. He could never imagine what it felt like to be a woman, a black woman, an unmarried pregnant black woman - assuming, she really was pregnant. He heard the TV in the living room and guessed that Tyra had found way to entertain herself.

Winn heard the toilet flush, the brief sound of water rushing from a tap, and then the door to the bathroom opened. Lonni leaned against the door frame and folded her arms across her chest. She looked at him and sighed.

"I'm pregnant."

Lonni

Lonni was not exactly sure what she needed. But she always knew what she wanted. So many pieces seemed to be missing, but she understood the extent of the pain she, Lonni Ava Simmons, had created on her own. Yet a part of her yearned for this pain, and she owned it.

Remaining in Philadelphia was a risk to some extent. Her parents Leon and Elaine had moved them from the hardscrabble Liberty City hood, like all parents of the time, in hopes of a better life for themselves and their children. They made that life in North Philly. By being careful and staying together, they succeeded. So, while her childhood seemed ideal, there was still something missing. What her parents had forgotten was to allow their children, all six of them, to be individuals. This oversight, however, was not inflicted by her father or her mother, but instead by her own burning desire for Winn's company. To be equal partners in all respects. Fear of being unprepared for the life deep in her womb frightened her.

"My mom said I could get new crayons today, and she gave me five dollars to buy them." Tyra's youthful innocence spoke of hope and promise to Lonni. She popped up every morning, prepared for another adventure that might unknowingly shape her own life in some way.

After one of Lonni's less stressful days at the office, her new neighbor, Angela, had convinced her to look after her daughter for a couple hours after school. Lonni could have refused, but Angela was recently divorced, and seemed like a nice person who just needed a little help. Although Tyra was an obedient child, after she had watched her a few times, she began to feel taken for granted. Angela presumed that Lonni was free. Not the case at all.

Although Lonni thought she knew what she wanted in life, at the same time things were suddenly more confusing. She drove to the CVS on Washington Avenue frustrated by the idea that she could be revealing a sad truth to herself - and aggravated by Angela's little ray of sunshine annoyingly swinging her feet in the backseat for free.

"Miss Laaaahni, did you hear me?"

"I'm sorry? Yes Miss Tyra. Remind me later, and we'll grab them on the way out." Lonni peered in her rearview to see a satisfactory smile of approval on Tyra's face.

The parking lot was half-full. The cool air of late September was perfumed by bistro and street smells. She saw that Winn had already arrived and hurriedly parked across from him. Lonni's heart raced. Right now, she was in a state of limbo. After they left CVS tonight, she would either be relieved or submerged into a deeper state of uncertainty.

There was not much to say to Winn now. In a way she blamed him. In other ways she blamed herself. "You should have been more forceful…used Plan B even…protection Lonni, what got into you?" Her thoughts were deafening loud again. She felt herself growing more reserved when it came to Winn. When they met, their love promised freedom of a sort, just the two of them. But they already had a scare. She hadn't told him, and fortunately, nothing had happened. Now they'd been together eighteen months. She did not want it then; what made her want it now? By the time she silenced herself for the hundredth time since stepping out of the car, Tyra had zoomed through the automatic CVS doors and over to the massive back-to-school Crayola display to choose how she'd spend her five-dollar fortune.

Lonni remained poised. She was very beautiful and knew it. She sometimes used her own beauty to get what she wanted. But she could confuse it for strength when it came to situations where a major choice was the subject. Lonni was not used making major decisions. While she thought she'd picked her college based on her family's lineage, really the decision was not hers at all. Her great grands, grandparents, parents and older brother had all attended the same school; and if she wanted her education paid for, she'd have to attend as well. Her parents even influenced her staying in Philadelphia. Family first. But what was her choice now?

She wished Winn would just buy it for her. She also wished she had come alone - without Tyra, without Winn, and without all the eyes in CVS secretly judging the three of them. It was already awkward enough because the six-year-old could have easily been their daughter. Lonni wanted to avoid claiming any children until she absolutely had to. In the Feminine Care section, she deliberated on which test kit was most accurate, and if a more expensive brand meant less false positives. Decisions! She finally closed her eyes and picked one.

At the register, the skinny cashier eyed them as if she'd never seen a couple purchase a pregnancy test before. Lonni felt eerily distant from Winn at that moment, and he looked a little like a child while reaching into his wallet to pay. Yes, he was two years younger than her, but in many ways, he seemed to be her elder. Only scanning beeps and register sounds broke the silence. Even Tyra was not speaking, having not found the right coloring implements to invest in.

"Have a good day," the cashier said, with a hint of sarcasm. She handed Winn the receipt as he took the bag. Lonni allowed Tyra to pay for what she had chosen, but Tyra was dissatisfied still. Lonni could not focus on the child's issue just then, which may have been selfish, but the subject of children had begun to loom over her more quickly than she thought. She was 27, and back in college she was always thought to be the first one who'd plummet headlong into motherhood. Instead, it seemed, she was coming in last.

The three of them caravanned back to Lonni's. Angela had called Tyra on their way home informing her that she'd have to stay with Miss Lonni a little longer this evening. Tyra burst out crying. Lonni had no clue how to respond - each of Tyra's tantrums were always soothed in a different manner depending on the infraction. Sometimes ignoring her worked, sometimes it didn't. Sometimes bribery worked, sometimes it didn't. Sometimes walking away worked, sometimes you were stuck in a car and couldn't do any of that.

She drove got home as quickly and safely as possible, all the while checking for Winn's Honda in the rearview mirror as her anxiety level grew. The plan was to get Tyra in front of a TV and get herself alone in the bathroom. After settling Tyra, Winn followed Lonni upstairs. As much as she outwardly despised the situation, she inwardly relished the power it gave her - the power to decide.

She locked the bathroom door behind her. Winn sat on her disheveled bed. Her thoughts raced as she prepared the test. She could feel Winn's desire for answers trying to burst through the door. She finished her contortions over the toilet, capped the stick, washed her hands, and stared blankly at herself through the mirror. The test lay face down on the countertop that was once part of her careful world. With each second, impatience grew. She paced in front of the sink. Barefoot, apprehensive and full of possibility. She knew the answer the Clear Response stick would give - what she did not know was her response. She flipped the test over before the results were ready at least three times, and on the fourth, the plus sign leapt off the stick and hit her square between the eyes. An inexplicable chill went through Lonni's body. She attempted to make sense of the shiver but got nothing. She was pregnant.

Tyra

The craft aisle at CVS was Tyra's favorite. It was as overwhelming as that of an office supply store and infinity more interesting than a grocery. She especially loved opening the packets of crayons and markers to test their brightness, fluidity and smells against one another. A CVS stock-boy in his employee smock walked into the aisle as she opened yet another pack of markers. They made eye contact for a few seconds, but he turned around and walked away.

While deciding which box of markers to pick, some movement in the next aisle caught her eye. Looking through a slot between items on the shelf, she could see Lonni on the other side. She was holding two boxes in her hands and Winn was standing very close to her. She couldn't hear exactly what was being said, but she knew it was an adult conversation that her mother would tell her to stay out of. But she couldn't help overhearing the word "pregnancy". That's a big word. She thought it had something to do with babies, and almost blurted out a question before realizing that she'd blow her cover. She often got scolded by her parents for wandering in the store alone.

"Is that your kid?" the store clerk said to Lonni, pointing his thumb to the right of him. "She's opening our merchandise." Tyra ducked down in her aisle, as if she was tall enough to be spotted over the shelving, trying to hide behind her box of markers.

"I'm sorry, sir, she must've lost me," Lonni said nonchalantly. She walked around the shelving and stood Tyra up with a disapproving glance. "Miss Cruz, please come with me," she said in her best principal voice. Then, holding her by the wrist, she led her toward the checkout.

At the counter, Tyra waited in line behind Lonni and Winn like an adult would, waiting to give the cashier her money and count the change like her mom had taught her to do. She took the five-dollar bill out and examined the fine print, sounding out words aloud as best she could. Her recitation was interrupted by Lonni and Winn arguing over which debit card the cashier should take.

"No take mine," Lonni was saying, but it was Winn who aggressively pushed his card toward the cashier.

Tyra squeezed in between the two and handed her five dollars to the clerk. "Just take mine!" She chimed in, which made all the adults laugh.

The clerk accepted Winn's card and Tyra's cash. He handed back her $2.38 change. She cupped her little hands together as she took the small pile of cash, then she dropped the thirty-eight cents into the cancer donation jar.

As they were walking to the car, Lonni and Winn were walking closely together but silent.

"Go ahead and get in Tyra," Lonni said pressing the key fob to unlock her car.

Tyra jumped into her booster seat in the back and fastened the seat belt. She saw Lonni and Winn exchanging words before Lonnie got into the car.

"I saw what you were holding in the store," said Tyra while Lonnie closed her door and buckled in. Lonni acted like she didn't know what Tyra was talking about. "You know, the pink box you were holding - it's my favorite color - can I see it?" Tyra thought she had bought crayons too.

"No, you can't." Lonni responded, a little exasperated.

"But boxes that color aren't for adults. Obviously. It's for a kid," Tyra explained, matter-of-factly.

Lonni tried to ignore her, looking at her through the rearview mirror, but curiosity got the better of her and she asked, "Okay, please explain to me how the color pink is for kids."

"Well, girl kids, anyway," Tyra corrected. "You know, it's like when you're a baby and they give girl kids a pink hat, just like I had. And Barbie likes pink, and little girls play with Barbie, and it's just a cute color. But adult girls like adult girl colors, like red. My mom wears red. Her lipstick is red, her purses are red, and even her bra is red. I can tell you one thing; my mom never washed any red underwear of my dad's."

"TYRA!" Lonni interrupted. She'd didn't like where this was going. Too much information from a six-year-old. Kids these days - they seem to know so much at such an early age. Lonni couldn't remember being like that. Would here own child be even more precocious?

These were the things that Lonni found annoying of Tyra. Of course, Tyra could trigger all the non-conservative views Lonni supported, like disassociating from people who used labels and gender-bias. For instance, there was the time that Tyra asked to see her closet. She then insisted that Lonnie was not a girly girl because she didn't own many dresses. Or even worse, Tyra once overheard Lonni and her mom talking about wanting to make Tyra a big sister very soon.

"What about you Lon?" Angela asked, "When are you thinking about settling down?" Lonni firmly explained that she did not want any babies.

"You don't want babies?" Tyra exclaimed as she walked around the corner to where her mother and Lonni sat. "You know you're supposed to have babies, right? You're a girl!"

That was the time Tyra learned to "stay out of grown folks' business."

The car drove on in silence, and Tyra began coloring with her new crayons in her book. She glanced up to see Lonni with a furrowed brow, as if she was thinking hard about something.

Tyra tried to guess. "So, is that guy your boyfriend?" she asked.

"What are boyfriends, Tyra?" Lonnie challenged.

"You know..."

Lonni sighed and rolled her eyes, turning up her music louder to block out any further inquiries from the backseat. Young Tyra had no clue why Lonni wasn't answering her questions like she usually would. Just then, Lonni's phone rang. She saw the ID, swiping right to answer before the voicemail did, while simultaneously extending the phone to Tyra.

"Here, it's your mom."

"Hey mom! I just bought my crayons and I counted the change too! But I gave some of it to the poor kids on the jar. I thought that would be nice!" Tyra spoke excitedly.

Moments later, however, Lonnie could see Tyra's face fall. She mumbled a few more words into the phone, then handed it back. "Ms. Lonni, my mom wants to speak with you."

Lonni took the phone back. Angela was informing her that she would to be late again tonight, and if Lonni could watch her for a little longer.

Tyra overheard Lonni's half of the conversation and asked, "Am I going home?"

"Not just yet. Your mom won't be back until later."

This news threw Tyra into a fit. She burst out in tears - screaming and yelling the rest of the ride home. Although she had quieted down some by the time they pulled into the driveway, Lonni still had to pry her from the booster seat. But Tyra's fit returned in all its glory once Lonni had her on her hip, resisting and kicking. By now, they both had enough.

Once inside Lonni's house, Tyra settled down. She threw her backpack on the floor and ran to the TV as fast as she could. She knew that her favorite cartoon will be on soon. At her house, every time she would come from school she would watch the same TV show and eat cereal while doing homework. She was content, at least for the moment, until her mom got back from work.

"Do you have any cereal?" Tyra asked. "My mom always give me cereal when I come home."

"Just a second. I will be right back," promised Lonni as she headed upstairs with Winn.

Twenty minutes passed, and Tyra got tired of watching TV. Now she wanted some cereal. She left the den and headed to the kitchen. She thought she was old enough to make cereal; she'd seen her mom do it all the time. While passing the stairway, she heard Lonni and Winn talking a bit loudly, much of which she couldn't make out. Curiosity got the better of her, and she proceeded up the steps to where the voices sounded clearer.

"Why are you acting so awkwardly, Lonni?"

"Me? No, it's how you think you control this situation that's awkward."

"What do you mean?"

"I just peed on a stick that I never thought I'd have to buy any time soon. Just the thought of waiting to see the verdict makes me feel anxious. I feel that I could be out of control like a baby in a few months. It's a feeling I don't want to have." Lonni poured out her soul. "I don't know how I feel at this point, Winn. I don't know if I have lived my life enough. I don't know if I'm ready to settle down. Our relationship hasn't even reached its potential yet. I don't even know how completely I feel about us co-parenting when our love is still so young - are we even in love, Winn?"

The room was engulfed in silence. Suddenly, Tyra felt a little guilty at the top of the stairs. She knew this was adult talk, and she'd better knock on the door and not barge right in because her mother taught her not to interrupt adults when talking. When Lonnie opened the door, Tyra could see Winn sitting on the edge of the bed, hands wedged between in legs, biting his lip and looking down at the floor.

"Can I have cereal now?" Tyra asked.

"What?! Oh, can you give us a second more?" Lonni asked. Glancing at Winn, she knelt and took Tyra's hands. "You're a big girl, right? Big girls make cereal..." she said, echoing the earlier conversation. "Go ahead and make yourself some, just don't make a mess. Okay?"

"Yes ma'am." Tyra went back downstairs to the kitchen. She looked in the pantry and didn't see any of the cereal she was used to eating, but she knew her grandma liked raisin bran, so she picked that. Then over to the refrigerator to get some milk, and a bowl from the dishwasher. She felt so grown up. She poured the cereal and milk together in a big bowl, splashing a little on the floor. When she was finished, she got up to put the milk back in the fridge.

Suddenly, a loud shout of "I'm pregnant!" from Lonni upstairs startled Tyra. She dropped the milk jug to the floor, spilling and splashing everywhere. Then a thud shook the walls as Tyra slipped on the vinyl and landed on her back. Lonni and Winn heard the commotion downstairs and ran to see what had happened.

Lonnie scooped Tyra up from the floor and cradled her in her arms. Although Tyra wasn't really hurt, she began to cry anyway as Lonni rocked her and asked her if she was okay. This was the first time the two of them had been so close, and Winn was there to observe how she soothed the child. Soon Lonni's racing heart returned to normal.

PART 2: GAME NIGHT

Winn

Leaving Mike's Coffee, Winn brushed by another couple coming in, and he hated Lonni again for cancelling on him. Saturday morning walks were supposed to be "their thing", but in the last five weeks, she'd only joined him once. It was slowly dawning on him that maybe walks were just HIS thing. As the first cool breezes of autumn began to swirl, he was grateful for the warm paper cup that gave him something to do with his hands.

He was already halfway to Lonni's before getting the text, so he decided to continue his walk alone. As he broke away from the sidewalk, and joined the path leading to one of the popular hiking trails in the city, he considered for a moment that this could be every Saturday morning for the rest of this life if Lonni left him. Alone on the trail on life. Maybe by then he'd have learned to walk unaccompanied; to just be a solo act. And maybe he wouldn't have the coffee either.

"I never know what to do with my hands," a seven-year-old Winn once complained to his mother when they were placing photos of his birthday party into an album.

She'd laughed, her broad shoulders rocking with every breath. "You'll learn, my love. You'll learn."

But no, after twenty-five years on this planet, he still hadn't. Now, he held the cup in both hands, close to his chest, letting the slow steam warm his face. Fellow hikers probably thought he was just an overgrown boy, afraid his cup was going to be taken from him. He dropped his hands and sighed. Looking up for the first time that morning, he noticed that the sky had changed from the azure of summer to a grayer blue. The expanse of trees before him stretched to the horizon, their shades of green just starting to be tinged with yellow and orange – the first hints of fall. He was reminded of the year's end closing in; and wondered if the time for his relationship with Lonni was running out as well.

Taking a sip of coffee, Winn smiled to himself. He'd read somewhere, in between processing checks at the office, that smiling more - to others and to yourself - changed your mood and gave a better outlook on life. He'd been practicing this for the past week, mostly to himself. He hadn't gained the courage to randomly smile at too many others yet. Sometimes it helped, sometimes it made him feel like a fool. Foolish. That was the word. That was how he felt this morning when Lonni cancelled, how he felt when looked up at that article at work to get out of a mid-day funk, how he felt now with his long arms dangling at his side, his hands heavy with fear, shame and guilt. He had barely spoken to Lonni since they found out she was pregnant. He knew what HE wanted, but he still wasn't sure how she felt.

Angela had invited them to game night tonight, so he planned to hash it out with her then. They needed to decide how to move forward.

A woman walked by with her dog and smiled at him, "Good morning."

"Hi." It came out sounding like a raspy whisper. By the time he cleared his throat and remembered to smile, she'd already passed by. *Foolish.*

Her perfume lingered behind and mixed pleasantly with the scents of the air and the trees. He wanted to follow her, to be a part of something new that she stirred in him. A part of her attraction was that her scent was like icing on a cake - adding to something that was already so perfect. To be in harmony with the space around you was a longing he's had for years; a longing he'd never put to words. Winn shook himself. *What was he thinking?* Here he had a pregnant girlfriend and he's looking at another woman. Maybe he wasn't ready for all of this. He feared that the imbalance and disparity he felt might become true.

He'd always known that everything about him seemed to be in conflict. While his friends had stopped growing in junior high, he continued to shoot to the sky, finally reaching 6'-4". But he felt ungainly; almost unsure of what to do with his long arms and legs. His height paired with his skin, a caramel color, made everyone in high school assume he was something he was not – a player, dishonest, unfriendly, uncouth.

Winn had to work hard for his friends in college. Freshmen didn't just walk up and ask him to shoot hoops, or go to the library, or to tonight's thing on fraternity row, like they did everyone else.

"I don't know, Winn, I guess you seem unapproachable," his roommate, Roger, had confessed to him in their junior year. "Everyone thinks you already have everything you need - money, smarts, looks, friends. So, they assume you don't need them. They don't even try."

He found the analysis unreasonable at the time, but now, five years later, he still pondered on it. He and Roger didn't remain friends. Nothing in particular had happened, it was just one of those relationships that dissolved seamlessly - the changes in space and time unable to sustain foundations that were once solid and impenetrable. He hadn't spoken to Roger since they graduated. Sometimes he couldn't even remember his face, his last name, nor half the things they did together. But those words, and the look in eyes as he delivered a message on behalf of what felt like the entire student body, would stay with him for the rest of his life.

Smile. It didn't work. He still felt foolish. After travelling for a year after college, he'd moved to Philadelphia and spent a year trying to nail down the "perfect job" while his parents supported him from afar. There's that money part Roger had mentioned. Eventually he began work as an accountant with Kindred Homes, a real estate company, that prided itself on placing families in a home where they can grow and thrive. Grow and thrive. Like Lonni's baby was doing at this very moment. Growing and thriving.

Winn tripped on a rock the size of his fist and cursed. He hadn't realized how fast he'd been walking. He looked at his fitness tracker. 6,234 steps. From his house to the coffee shop to here. Wherever here was. He'd walked the trail a few times before, but that was months ago. When it was a different season and the trees were greener and the sky was bluer. He was hoping to rediscover the path with Lonni this morning. Hoping that it would get them talking again. Hoping that it would help her remember what it was like with just the two of them. Hoping that it would get them back in their routine and some sense of normalcy. Then he remembered that the walking ritual was his routine, never hers. *Foolish.*

Another game night. Winn hated them with a passion. He'd spent the day organizing and reorganizing his apartment - when he felt his life tumult, keeping busy helped him feel more in control of things. Every game night ended with him feeling embarrassed, ignorant, or just like a complete idiot. Taboo was too difficult; Charades was confusing; Mafia was drawn out and complex; and Trivial Pursuit gave him anxiety. But tonight, he needed to focus on just him and Lonni, and coming to some consensus about their baby.

When he arrived that evening, Lonni was already sitting on the couch, a sparkling water in one hand, making small talk with other guests. They were laughing at something she'd said. Normally he would greet her with a kiss as he sat next to her, and maybe took a sip of her drink. He'd tell a joke and put his arm around her as she continued to talk. He longed for the days of just a month ago and regretted that he had ever taken that normal for granted. She looked at him and he smiled at her while motioning to the back of the house. She didn't return his smile, but she got up and he was grateful for that.

"Let's talk in the backyard," she said leading the way. Winn followed, walking past a large man gnawing at a chicken wing while reading the back of a cardboard game box. He realized that he hadn't met the host nor had Lonni attempted to introduce him. She led him through the kitchen where the large grey-tiled island was covered by food trays and wine bottles. Half a dozen people were in the room pulling even more food out of the oven and microwave and grabbing items from refrigerator. They poured themselves drinks while reconnecting with one another.

Lonni walked past them and opened a sliding glass door that led to the patio. Another couple had beat them there, sitting on two chaises, foreheads almost touching, whispering. Winn was immediately jealous. He hadn't experienced that type of intimacy with Lonni in a long time. They headed across the lawn to a swing set on the far end of the yard.

Finally, alone together, he looked critically at her. "So, how've you been? We haven't really talked much."

"I've been ok. Confused mostly." She was looking down at the grass.

"Do you know what you want to do?"

"No." It was almost a whisper. "Do you?"

"Yes."

She looked at him, her eyes desperately searching his for a clue. "It's not that easy for me," she said, finally. Her hands moved into her back pockets. Classic nervous Lonni move.

"Well, shouldn't we talk this through?" Winn felt himself growing anxious.

"No…I mean, yes. I don't know. It's hard to talk to you about this."

"Why? I don't understand."

"I don't either," she shrugged.

This was proving to be more difficult than he expected. He came here to engage in a fruitful conversation and leave with a decision. But here she was, telling him that she couldn't even speak to him and she didn't know why. Roger's words came back to mind. *They don't even try.*

"Lonni, I need to know how I can help you and support you in this." He put his hands on her shoulders and ignored the fact that he felt her tense up at the move. "This is happening to me too, you know?"

"You have no idea what this is like." She shook her head.

"Then tell me!"

She looked away, towards the couple that was now locked in an embrace and kissing.

Suddenly, a light shone on the grass before them. Winn looked up and saw that a light in the window overseeing the yard had been switched on. The smooching couple briefly broke apart, laughed lightly, and got back to it. The light remained on, and he wondered who was up there. Was the host taking a break from the crowd in her home? Was a guest snooping around, maybe at first innocently looking for the bathroom and then stumbling upon the master bedroom instead? He looked down at Lonni again. Her petite figure seemed even smaller than he remembered. And she looked exhausted.

"How have you been, you know, health-wise?"

"I'm ok. Just nauseous and a little uncomfortable." She looked off into the distance and laughed. "It feels like I'm sick you know? Like I have the flu and won't go away." He nodded even though he didn't know. He could never know. Her voice suddenly increased, "I know you want to resolve this right now. But I can't give that to you, Winn."

"Why?"

"I don't know! I just don't know. And the pressure from you. The calls. The texts. The stupid walks! None of that is going to make me want to keep or not keep this baby!"

"Woah, slow down..."

"You're making this harder for me," she protested.

"Lonni, you're being difficult."

"I need space…"

"Wait a minute."

"No. I'm not doing this with you!" Lonni stormed towards the sliding door and, after a brief battle with it, yanked it open and went in without bothering to shut it behind her. The other couple was sitting up now. They were holding hands and he could feel them staring at him. He couldn't see their faces, but he didn't need to. Had it been him watching instead, emotions ranging sympathy, embarrassment, and possibly disgust would have registered on his. He hated that Lonni had put him in this position - the position of the guy that slowly walked after the girlfriend through a crowded home desperately trying to get away from him. He hated it, yet he followed her in.

The crowd in the kitchen had doubled in size and he wondered how long they'd been out there. Most of the food had been moved into the living room, but people remained around the island - some sitting on it now - discussing events of the week, upcoming vacations, that cute thing their daughter did yesterday, and how to savor that now because they're not so cute when they become teenagers.

Winn pushed past them towards the living room where a lively game of Charades was in full swing. A woman was leaping around the room, her index fingers pointing up on both sides of her head, while one side of the room aggressively yelled out every animal name known to man. A quick look revealed that Lonni was not there.

He walked outside and looked across the street toward Lonni's house. The light in her foyer was on. She was back at home. Winn desperately wanted to follow her. To demand to be heard; to command her to speak; to will her to love him enough to trust him with her decision. But he was exhausted, both physically and mentally. He was totally drained by the hike, the cleaning, and now this. Dejectedly, he sunk into his Honda and drove home, unsurprised that though he had not participated in a single game tonight, he still left with those same feelings of shame and defeat.

Lonni

Lonni slept late on Saturdays, ignoring the sun shining brightly through her blinds. It was the weekend, and there was no need for the alarm clock. She knew Winn would be mad at her missing another chance to take a walk through the city. It was a sweet gesture, but they would have countless opportunities to take that walk as a family, maybe sooner than later. It wasn't that morning walks through the brisk fall air with a warm, sweet cup of Mike's coffee were unpleasant. Whether they spent their waking moments together or not, they were connected.

Lonni excelled at so many things - hiding her emotions for the sake of others happened to be a specialty. Part of her understood that soon she might no longer be entitled to her own freedom. But instead of hashing it out with Winn, she only acknowledged her concerns inwardly. It gnawed at her until she picked up her phone and gave him a call.

"Hey." Winn sounded as if he had recently come out of a deep thought himself.

"Hi, it's me. I know you aren't going to want to hear this, but I won't be able to make it over to Mike's this morning. I really need to go by the doctor for a check-up."

Who was Winn to argue with that? "Okay, but why didn't you tell me you were going? Don't you want me there with you? You know I would've gone." His tone expressed disappointment, and she could feel it.

"I just want to handle this myself, Winn. There'll be plenty more doctor visits, so don't worry about missing this one." She started to hang up. Explaining why she hadn't invited him was too difficult. She just hadn't - it was her choice. "I'm sorry I missed Mike's with you. Anyway, I'm about to jump in the shower, and my appointments an hour. I'll call you afterwards. Okay?"

"Okay, Lonni. Call me when you need me, I guess." The phone hung up immediately.

Lonni slowly rose from her bed after contemplating the conversation. She pulled the curtains back allowing the full sun to enter and made her way to the bathroom. Dark brown curls coiled slightly from under her night scarf as she peered at herself in the mirror. She sighed. *The only way you'll be content with this choice is if you make it work for you.* Tonight, she was expected to decide. A decision that would not only impact herself, and Winn, but a new life that neither of them were prepared for.

She showered and dressed as thoughts swirled around her head. She caressed her belly, examining it to see if changes were already happening as she prepared for her first appointment. She shook her head at the thought of Winn, because she wished things between them were as simple as they once were. Happiness in her world turned to heaviness in so many ways. Meanwhile Angela and Tyra were coercing her and Winn to participate in a game night at the same time. She was consumed by stress. The decision whether to protect what she and Winn created was one that needed to be resolved, and soon. Either way, they'd have plenty to talk about this evening.

Lonni and dusk arrived at the party at the same time. While Winn was on his way, she had enough time to get acquainted with everyone else at the gathering. She was blessed with a certain charisma that had served her well throughout life. From college, to work, and at social events, she always knew what to do and say in social settings. And normally she loved game nights. Tonight, however, she was not in the mood for the loud exchanges on who was right, wrong or cheated, and uninterested in hearing someone incorrectly explain the rules to Yahtzee. *Who still played Yahtzee, anyway?*

Couples mingled around the townhouse together, laughing with other couples, looking at each other like couples, sitting like couples. Lonni was overwhelmed with emotion because she wanted Winn and wanted to be alone at the same. She poured herself a glass of sparkling water, squeezed lime juice into it, then decorated the glass with the fruit rind before sitting quietly on a couch in the living room. She steeled herself to engage in conversation and dodge any questions that might get too personal.

Tyra bounced around the party, asking questions and doling out compliments, and found happiness in the mere fact that people were in her house during her bedtime. Free. Tyra was free. She represented everything that Lonni always wanted, to be free of what anyone else thought, influenced solely by her own choices. And in some way, Tyra also represented the beautiful child who might someday be her own, with Winn, and could be influenced by her love. She resented herself for seeing the innocent truth through a little one who lived with no regrets because it was not Tyra's fault she was free. And it was not Tyra's fault that Lonni battled with the idea that she may have lost her own freedom.

Winn finally arrived, and by then, at least twenty others were there, laughing and talking loudly. She caught Winn's glance as he smoothly strolled over to where she'd been seated and greeted her with a smile.

The times where he'd wrap his arms around her seemed like the distant past. Now she felt a little awkward in his presence.

"Hi…How are you…I'm fine." They spoke and replied simultaneously.

"I'm good," Winn finally spoke alone, "You look nice."

"Thanks, you do too."

He nodded at her glass. "Wanna refill?"

"Sure. Just a water is fine."

"Okay, lets grab it and go outside then, it's a little loud in here."

Lonni fluttered internally as she led him outside to talk. Her thoughts whirled as they made their way through the small crowded kitchen. She began to reflect while fixing the drinks. *Lonni, don't bring it up. This is not the time to have a conversation that takes real thought. If he asks, just say "Later."* It was apparent that he noticed changes in her. Winn looked down at her small frame and could sense the heaviness Lonni spoke of when describing the symptoms that she experienced. It had been at least a week since they had confirmed the pregnancy, and even longer since they had spent intimate time together, just being a couple. But Lonni now longed for that aloneness - their child would soon be accompanying her every second of everyday.

Once they were in the backyard, Lonni saw that another her couple was already on the patio, and she could tell they were in love. Compared to them, it seemed as if she and Winn had only been acting until now. While tensions were never high between them, today they were. She looked at Winn, and with each glance, she wanted more and more for this situation to disappear. She was frustrated. She wanted to look to Winn for answers, but he was looking to her. The way the situation was unraveling, someone needed to say a prayer for them.

Winn had come the party with the express desire to learn her decision. All she wanted was to not be forced. He had this way about him that could convince her almost of anything, so she tried to prepare for his coming persuasions.

"Lonni, why is it so difficult for us to talk now? I'm tired of not being able to communicate like adults, to come to some conclusion. Since finding out you're pregnant, you don't want to talk to me. You seem distant. Don't you want this?"

"Winn, pleeeease. Don't get all dramatic on me right now. I want this. I really do. But I hate the fact that you have no idea what I'm going through."

"So, you've made up your mind?"

"I DON'T KNOW WINN! I don't have an answer. At least not yet. This situation is bigger than us, bigger than me at least. Winn…don't you understand that?"

"C'mon, Ava," he said sarcastically, using her middle name like her mom did when she was in trouble. "Do you have any idea what has been going on in my head? The woman I love has a part of me growing inside, and I don't think she wants anything to do with it." He glared at her.

"I have to go Winn. This is not the time, nor the place." She turned back toward the house and he followed. She had some pride and didn't want strangers eavesdropping, hoping to catch a juicy tidbit of their conversation.

"No, you're going to talk to me. I deserve that much." She slipped through the door and Winn thought he might as well be speaking to the wind. The in-love couple looked on and embraced one another tighter, happy that their relationship had not yet produced such trying times.

Once inside again, Winn discovered that she had already left for home and fell silent. He looked out the living room window and saw the light from Lonni's porch shining between them. He thought he made out a shadow looking back at him before disappearing inside.

Lonni stood behind the curtains of her front window with her arms crossed, wishing that he'd come sweep here away, making her safe from her uncertainty tonight. Instead they had come to an impasse. Her only company tonight would be the developing baby who was now hers.

She watched through the window as he climbed into his car and slowly drove off, continuing to look until the taillights of his Accord could no longer be seen.

Tyra

"Okay, girl, it's about your bedtime." Angela guided her daughter down the hallway to her bedroom. Later, Tyra would be allowed to "play" with the grown-ups for a little while. And she was entertaining! A well-behaved child, she would mingle and dance with the guests who were always happy to oblige her.

Back in her bedroom, amidst the faint sounds of laughter and old-time music beating through her door, Tyra pulled out her favorite Barbie doll. It was the one who worked as a Therapist from nine to five. There she sat in her little house playing God, working through all the problems of Barbie's only patient, Ken, while wiping away his imaginary tears as he lay on the plastic sofa explaining his issues. She pursed her lips to imitate a high voice that brought Barbie to life.

"I can fix your problems, Ken," she said sweetly.

In response, she was ready rumble her throat to give the best man's voice she could muster. She took a deep breath, but before she could speak, she heard, "I can't take this any longer!" from a loud voice outside her window.

Tyra peered up from her playhouse as she heard a perfect imitation of Ken from her window pane. Out of curiosity, she clocked out of work and jumped up from her doll house, heading to the window. Pressing her freckled faced against the glass, she used her tiny hands like binoculars to block the light from her bedroom, so she could see clearly into her backyard. Lonni and Winn were there.

They were talking to face to face, and Tyra couldn't hear much behind her glass window but could tell they were having argument.

Lonni threw her arms up in frustration with Winn as she walked away from him, turning toward the house to rejoin the party. Tyra tried to pull her sticky face from the window to get back to work before Barbie noticed her absence, but Winn saw her, and he instantly regretted everything he said to Lonni. Tyra went back to her dollhouse, apologizing to Ken for neglecting his concerns.

She heard the back door of her house slam as Winn angrily reentered. She looked down at herself, at her white polka dot pajamas, and asked Barbie if she wants to play dress up. She and Barbie decided they wanted to be dancers that night. She pulled together her best leotard and tutu, so she and Barbie could closely match, and spun and twirled to the music still pounding against her door. She unraveled the long French braid her mother had committed to weaving every night to tame her wildly curly brown hair. She knew it would make Ken happy.

After falling to the ground in laughter from her dizzy performance, she heard her favorite Marvin Gaye song that played at every family event. That was her signal to come out and entertain, and she burst through her bedroom door with excitement. In the living room, everyone was gathered around her in joy, except Winn who was sitting on the sofa staring at his knees. Lonnie was nowhere in sight and must have already gone home. She ran and pulled Winn by the arm, forcing him to stand and smile. However, he soon excused himself and left for the evening. Tyra continued to dance in circles, raving the on lookers, but even in her youth, she could tell something was amiss.

PART 3: THE REVEAL

Winn

Winn Justice James was born into a Christian family, and while his faith had always been a large part of his formative years, he admittedly never fully understood it or how its precepts could apply to his adult life. Instead, he struggled with it. He struggled with the spiritual disciplines - the praying, the quiet time with a God he could neither see nor hear, the reading of what he perceived to be "an outdated text irreverent to the time" that he was living in now.

So, it came as a surprise that immediately after he received Lonni's text about meeting at Mike's to discuss the baby, he got on knees and prayed. He prayed for forgiveness - for the things he had done and the things he was about to do. He prayed for Lonni, that she would be at peace with his decision and that she would be at peace with hers. And most of all, he prayed that they would want the same thing. It was hypocritical, the whole thing. But this thing was all he had so he did it anyway, hoping against hope that somehow it would work.

Winn drove to Mike's Coffee and ordered a large black coffee with a lemon scone. He picked a window table that was close enough to the exit, should Lonni decide to make a scene, but far enough for her to think twice before storming out.

When she arrived, she appeared to be in a better mood than the last time he saw her at game night last week. A full week. The pregnancy had to be at least month and a half along by now. They were running out of time.

"How've you been?" Lonni asked. She was wearing a light pink lip gloss, the only makeup she had on.

"I'm good," he smiled, "I'm glad you texted. I'm glad you want to talk."

"Yes, we need to."

"Do you want anything?"

"Um, no I'm fine. I can't keep anything down." She touched her stomach.

"I'm sorry." There was a long pause as they looked at each other.

Finally, Lonnie drew a breath and said, "I don't know. I guess I don't want to be alone in this decision."

Her words stung. "I'm not going anywhere Lonni. You know that."

"Well, you haven't made that clear in the last couple of weeks."

"Mostly because you haven't given me a chance…"

She raised her hand to silence him. "I don't want to fight. Not today." She sounded resigned and almost as emotionally exhausted as he was. He reached across the table and took her hands.

"Then what DO you want?"

She looked at him again, searching his eyes, preparing an answer. In his peripheral vision Winn saw two people walking purposely towards them. He turned and saw it was Lonni's neighbor and her daughter – *Myra?*

"Hi, Lonni!" the girl squealed.

Lonni smiled and said, "Hiya, Tyra," causing the girl to giggle again.

Tyra - that was it, thought Winn. Lonni extended her arms and the girl flew into them.

The woman introduced herself as Angela and apologized that she didn't have a chance to meet him at game night. "Regardless, I hope you had fun?"

He recalled the image of Lonni, shoving her hands in her pockets, looking at the floor, walking through the sliding door. He smiled weakly, "Yeah, it was great."

Lonnie and her neighbors continued to chat like he wasn't there. He looked at the girl and wondered if her mother had once contemplated keeping her. He wondered what value this girl would add to her family, her community, the world, and if any other decision would have taken something away from the world that was meant to be. He overheard Lonni discussing potential changes her in her schedule and possible babysitting time. Tyra looked at him and smiled. *Smile.*

Winn smiled back and immediately the little imp snatched his scone and put it in a hand behind her back. He looked at her mother and she hadn't noticed a thing. She was fully engaged in her conversation with Lonni. He looked at Tyra again and she smiled devilishly. It would be awkward asking a child to give back a $4 scone that she'd already touched. He'd look like a bully, or a snob almost, who couldn't even relinquish a cheap pastry for a child.

He stared at her and she stared back at him. Her brown eyes exposed him, his hypocrisy, his anxiety, his need to control, his decision. Her eyes told him his choice was selfish; that he was not considering Lonni, and that he was making a mess that he then expected God to clean up - the same God he had always cared less about. The locking of eyes was disquieting, and he looked away.

Tyra slowly moved her hand to her mouth and began eating the scone, looking at him the whole time, like a dare. Her mother looked down at her, and noticing nothing wrong, continued to talk with Lonni. *What are they saying and why is it taking so long?*

She finished the scone, the corners of her mouth lined with crumbs of evidence, and right on cue, the women finished their conversation, said their goodbyes, and left.

"What was that about?" he asked Lonni.

"She just needed help with somethings. I see you were getting along with Tyra." Winn shrugged. He did not want to think about that child again.

"I heard you say that your schedule's changing?"

"Yes", she looked down at the table and back at him, "That's what I wanted to talk to you about. That's why I wanted us to meet here."

"Okay." His pulse quickened. Here it comes.

Lonni shifted in her seat as if to get more comfortable, moved his coffee cup off to the side, and took his hands into hers.

Lonni

Uncertainty had been Lonni's constant companion for the past month. But now she knew what must be done. She'd meet Winn, and they would decide on this baby, once and for all. Lately, instead of growing together, it seemed they were growing apart by the day. Lonni's mind raced with possible outcomes of this meeting, and all her plans might go up in smoke depending on what they decided today at Mike's.

Lonni prayed. She prayed often, but today she prayed more. Not only because she was uneasy about it all, but *they* had one to make. Winn hadn't made it obvious on whether keeping the baby was what he wanted, and she knew she hadn't made that obvious either. But she knew Winn and suspected that he'd want to keep it. Their life had grown increasingly difficult since finding out about the new addition. If she kept it, what should tell everyone around her? If she didn't, what guilt would haunt her? A decision had to be made - today and together. There was no way for them to avoid the elephant in the room any longer.

She sent him a meetup text. It was at Mike's they'd first met. Over coffee and pastries, a bond was formed. It was the ideal spot to help reignite the fire that was seemingly put out by the baby. When she arrived, Winn was already there at a table. That looked promising. Lonni was more relaxed today. In fact, she was prepared for whatever the response she got from him, based on her own decision. Hopefully, they'd match.

Black coffee, lemon scone. Winn only ordered a few things from the menu and that was his usual combination. As she sat, he offered to buy her something, but she declined - her stomach was already a little queasy. At that moment, Winn looked like everything she had always wanted.

Tall stature, growing seniority in his business, a focus on her, and willingness to make things work out. And she was all he desired, just not to the extent that she had let him in.

Across from each other, the warm ambience of the cafe setting the tone, she stared into his eyes as the conversation unfolded. Soon, her hands were in his.

"What do you really want, Lonni?"

She searched his eyes, and he was staring back intently. As she began to part her lips to say his name, a familiar voice rang in her ear.

"Hi, Miss Lonni!" Tyra was overflowing with excitement from running into them.

"Hiya, Tyra," Lonni cracked a genuine half-smile and leaned over to hug the little girl from her seat. She began to wonder if each time she needed to make a major decision involving her child, Tyra would pop into the room with pure her childlike innocence to bring happiness to everyone. Maybe it was karma.

Lonni and Tyra's mother, Angela, spoke for some time. Enough time for Lonni to watch Tyra take Winn's scone, hide it behind her back, and then devour it right in front of him. Winn hadn't retaliated in the least bit, letting the girl have the entire scone without telling her mother. Lonni was uncertain on whether this was commendable of him or not. She would have said something to Angela about Tyra's behavior.

"Yes, my schedule at the office will be changing soon for a few weeks. I'll let you know what things look like on my end once this project is over." The news wasn't entirely good, and Lonni hoped to move the duo along after learning this. She glared at Tyra who smiled broadly with her lemon scone coated lips, self-satisfied by her plundering ways. They shortly moved on.

"Children are so sneaky today," observed Lonnie.

"They really are." Winn replied, bringing them back to the real situation at hand. "She just ate my entire scone!" They chuckled. Ten minutes had elapsed since her arrival, and it was time to address the real matter.

Lonni closed her eyes and took a deep breath. She could feel him gazing deeply into her. This was it. Whether or not Winn agreed, she'd be delivering the final decision now. They were running out of time. She moved his coffee cup aside and took his large hands into her own. She searched his eyes again for signs that he'd understand her choice. Almost overcome by her self-induced stress, she caressed the outside of his hand, squeezed gently, and parted the lips that would soon break one of their hearts.

Tyra

Sunday's were Tyra's favorite. It was the day she and her mother spent time together after the busy work week ended. Her mom spent the day off gardening, watering the rose bushes, and everything in between. Tyra would wait inside patiently; ready to have fun with her mother once everything is done. Things like cooking Sunday dinner or decorating a cake her mom had baked from scratch - only to be devoured over the coming week. She loved looking outside the window at her mom grooming the yard.

Then, after she was bored, Tyra would go outside and pretend she was helping with the curb appeal. But instead of using garden tools or any dangerous equipment, she'd proceed with chalk. Her mother had a green thumb, and Tyra thought she was good at flowers too! She thought she was so good, that she drew them all over the concrete sidewalk and onto the driveway. Everything that she could think to make the house look pretty. Then she looked at happily at herself, because the chalk dust covering made her pretty as well, so she decided to draw herself and her mom. But she soon realized that that all her colors had been used up drawing flowers. All she had left was red, so red it was, all over the sidewalk.

"I'm gonna drop by Mike's Coffee after I get some more seeds from the florist. Do you want anything babe?" Tyra's mom asked.

"Can't I come, mommy?" Tyra called back.

"Yes, you may, but you're not getting in my car like that!"

Angela pulled the water hose over toward Tyra. She gently sprayed the cool water down her daughter's outstretched arms and hands, rinsing the red from her skin. Then she told Tyra to shake herself dry. She didn't need to be told twice. Tyra was soon flapping and gyrating like she was at a disco.

Her mom stood by admiring the artwork. "Oh, Tyra, is this us you drew? That's a pretty picture, but why did you only use red?"

"I ran out of chalk. Can we by some after we get coffee?"

"You mean, after 'I' get coffee?" Angela corrected. "The last thing you need is caffeine." Her mom laughed as Tyra skipped to the car, pretending she knew what that meant.

As the two of them proceeded down the street, Tyra saw Lonni coming out of her front door, stopping briefly to look at the mural on the driveway. Lonni seemed to admire it, but then she turned around with her head down and got in her car.

Syllble Writer Biography

Taiwo Adesina

After she came close to winning a spelling bee in the third grade, Taiwo Adesina has dedicated her life to the mastery, compilation and sharing of words through descriptive story-telling. Originally from California, Taiwo has a passion for using words to describe some of her wild experiences ranging from shark cage diving in South Africa, to Peace Corps in Senegal to zip-lining in Honduras. She doesn't believe a picture is worth a thousand words, she believes a thousand words are. Until she can live on a beach, write novels and eat pizza every day, Taiwo spends her days working in international development, supporting public health and nutrition programs around the world. She currently lives in Washington DC with her running shoes, Mac Book, Moleskin journals and Thesaurus. Read more about her journey and thoughts at travelgiveworklove.wordpress.com

Valeria Lake

Valeria Lake is a visionary. While she calls Atlanta, Georgia home, she is a native of Miami by way of Ocala, Florida. Valeria thrives when opportunities of creativity arise and enjoys seizing these projects with an open mind and fresh ideas. When she is not writing, you may catch her developing a brand or concept, planning a major event in her city, or fixing technological issues for Apple users across the globe. She is a risk taker, student to life, and lover of all things write!

Brittney Jones

Apart from daydreaming her life away, Brittney Jones makes her wildest dreams a reality – some through writing of course. Raised in Orlando, FL, Brittney was fond of the diverse inner-city and tourism culture. While attending Title I public schools throughout her adolescence, she was inspired by her 11th grade AP Language Arts teacher who expressed to the at-risk youth how important writing and effective communication was when trying to make a mark in such unfortunate circumstances. It was through these 'circumstances' where she enjoyed the craft of imagination and bringing those ideas to life through writing, especially targeting diverse groups and unpopular opinions/lifestyles. Today, Brittney is a self-proclaimed "creative" who is attentively invested in telling her imaginative stories in all forms of art medium.